# GLORIA RAND

# SALTY TAKES OFF

## Illustrated by TED RAND

Henry Holt and Company / New York

To Gloria's sister Dorothy Kistler

Special thanks to:
Lloyd Jarman, pioneer Alaskan pilot
and noted aviation historian;
and Cliff Hudson, pilot,
Hudson Air Service, Talkeetna, Alaska

Text copyright © 1991 by Gloria Rand
Illustrations copyright © 1991 by Ted Rand
First Edition
Published by Henry Holt and Company, Inc.,
115 West 18th Street, New York, New York 10011.
Published simultaneously in Canada by Fitzhenry & Whiteside Ltd.
195 Allstate Parkway, Markham, Ontario L3R 4T8.

Library of Congress Cataloging-in-Publication Data
Rand, Gloria.
    Salty takes off / Gloria Rand : illustrated by Ted Rand.
    Summary: While wintering in Alaska, Salty the dog falls from an
airplane and must survive until his master Zack finds him.
    ISBN 0-8050-1159-5
    1. Dogs—Juvenile fiction. [1. Dogs—Fiction. 2. Alaska—
Fiction.]   I. Rand, Ted, ill.   II. Title.
PZ10.3.R167Sal   1991
[E]—dc20       90-46371

Henry Holt books are available at special discounts
for bulk purchases for sales promotions, premiums,
fund-raising, or educational use. Special editions
or book excerpts can also be created to specification.

Printed in the United States of America
on acid-free paper. ⊗

10  9  8  7  6  5  4  3  2  1

# SALTY TAKES OFF

$\mathbb{W}$inter is no time to be out at sea in a boat the size of ours. We're laying over until spring," Zack told his crew, Salty Dog, as he eased their sailboat up to the moorage of a small town on the Gulf of Alaska.

While Zack packed up life vests, foul-weather gear, and extra provisions, Salty stayed inside. As a light snow began to fall, he barely poked his nose out to watch Zack stow away sails and cover the boat with a protective canvas.

"I'm counting on you to toughen up and brave the cold like a true Alaskan," Zack laughed. "Come on—we're going ashore to find warmer winter quarters."

Salty didn't stop shivering until he and Zack entered the steamy Golden Nugget Café.

"Well, well, well. New in town?" a cheerful customer asked as he bent down and brushed snow off Salty's head.

"We plan to spend the winter here." Zack introduced himself and his crew.

"My name's Jarman Curtis," the man said, grinning. "I run a flying service. Not many roads in Alaska—lots of folks get around by plane. Need a ride, just let me know."

"Thanks," Zack replied. "We'll remember that."

The next day Zack and Salty moved into their winter home, a real log cabin.

Salty explored every corner. He sniffed around the woodpile for mice, growled at an Indian mask, and barked at an ancient bearskin rug. Then he flopped down in front of the crackling fire and fell fast asleep.

Early the following morning Zack and Salty hiked out to the nearby airfield, where Jarman put Zack to work right away.

As the weeks passed, Salty grew a thicker coat. It helped keep him warm, but not warm enough to like being out in the cold hangar, where Zack repaired planes. Whenever he got the chance, Salty would sneak into the airfield's offices and snuggle up to the warm oil heater.

"Hey, you shouldn't stay inside so much," Jarman teased Salty. "You'll miss learning about Alaska. Want to go flightseeing?"

Salty looked doubtful as he trotted across the icy field to Jarman's plane, but he was happy sitting in the plane's heated cockpit.

"Hold on, Salty!" Jarman yelled over the roaring engine as they sped full speed down the runway and up into the clouds in a daredevil climb. This was fun!

Salty liked to fly. He and Jarman flew over wilderness lakes, large glaciers, and jagged mountains. They soared above low foothills where caribou, moose, and wolves lived. Once, they banked close to a steep, rocky slope to see a family of mountain goats. Harder to spot were deer and bear, but Salty kept a sharp lookout.

"Not so lonesome with you along," Jarman told Salty.

Salty was a good copilot and flew with Jarman nearly every day.

Together they made regular mail runs and delivered supplies to mines. They took equipment out to logging camps and food to tiny villages.

While Jarman checked off orders and unloaded the plane, Salty was always busy visiting new friends.

"Gotta make an emergency run," Jarman told Salty one morning. "They need a new part for their generator out at my village. They're stuck with no heat and no lights. Let's go!"

Salty ran out and hopped up into the plane.

The forecast was poor, and as the weather became stormier, the little plane bounced wildly up and down, dipping sharply from side to side. Salty was frightened. He scrambled toward the safety of Jarman's lap and was thrown against the cabin door. He caught his paw on the handle, and the door popped open.

Salty tumbled out into space!

Down, down, down he went.

With a thump Salty landed in thick
brambles covered with snow. He rolled over
and over until he found footing on firmer
ground. Then he stood up and began to
bark.

A ptarmigan, dressed in its white winter
feathers, took off in startled flight. A
snowshoe rabbit, wearing its white winter
fur, hopped quickly into another patch of
bushes.

Salty shook snow from his coat and barked
some more.

Then all was quiet, and Salty found himself
alone in a strange world.

Salty plowed through the snow as best he
could, first in one direction, then back
another way, stopping to listen, pausing to
look. What should he do now?

Finally, exhausted, he burrowed down into
the snow to rest and protect himself from
the cold.

Early the next morning Salty awoke to clear
skies and the familiar drone of an engine.
He was cold to the bone, hungry, and tired,
but he leapt up barking.

He barked and barked as loudly as he could
at the circling plane.

The pilot spotted Salty. The plane made
one more turn, then came down nearby,
landing smoothly on its skis.

Zack jumped out of the plane and stumbled toward his dog.

Salty bounded through the snow toward his master.

"Oh, Salty, my crew, my pal!" Zack cried out as he scooped up the happy dog. "Jarman told me we'd find you. He promised that you'd be okay. He was right!"

"Hey, fella, glad to see ya." Jarman gave Salty a big hug. "What a survivor you are!"

As Zack bundled Salty into an extra-warm parka, Salty wiggled all over. He was just about the happiest dog you could ever hope to see.

"Have a good hot dinner ready for Salty," Jarman ordered back to town over the plane's radio. "Something special. We're headed in, be there shortly."

When they landed, Salty was not eager to get out of the plane.

"Can't say as I blame him," Zack laughed as he patted the ground, encouraging Salty to jump. "See, Salty—it's not like the last time you went out that door. It's not far down at all."

"Come on, fella. It's okay," Jarman coaxed.

Salty jumped and everyone cheered.

"You're one tough flyer who braved the cold." Zack saluted Salty. "But it's time to report aboard ship. We're sailing soon for warmer waters."

With Zack close behind, Salty raced back to their boat, ready to return to sea, a true salty dog.